To James, Harriet

"Never stop dreaming"

SOCRATES

THE SPRINTING SNAIL OF SORRENTO

George G. Burton

Illustrated by Elaine Mathewson Falconer

George Burton

ISBN: 978-1491089828

Printed by Createspace, an Amazon Company

To the snail we saw on the window of the
Regina Hotel in Sorrento.

Without you, this book would not have
been written.

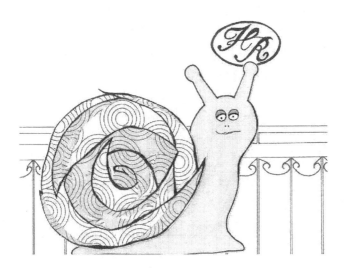

Introduction

We met Socrates at breakfast one morning. When we sat down at our table in the corner, he was outside on the window. I can only suppose that, after a long, long time living on the ground, dashing around doing all sorts of snaily things, Socrates had decided that he needed a holiday. A bit like us I suppose. Anyway, he decided that he would go north for a while, so he slithered out from under the fridge on the balcony outside the breakfast room, chose the biggest, cleanest, most sparkly window he could find and started off on the long journey up to the roof.

You might think that such a huge trip would take a snail for ever to complete, but don't forget, that he was Socrates the famous sprinting snail of Sorrento.

He set off at muesli time today, by scrambled eggs time he had climbed halfway, by crusty bread and coffee time he was three-quarters up the window, and by the time we got up to leave the breakfast table he had made it all the way to the ceiling. Perhaps he was going to send us a postcard describing the weather and other details once he got out onto the roof and got himself some rays of sunshine. He gave a final twitch of his feelers, unsucked his suckers and disappeared above the window frame.

Chapter 1

Socrates looked down from the roof of his hotel. What a beautiful sight it was! In the distance the deep blue of a perfect November sky met the green of the Mediterranean Sea in a straight line that was the horizon. He couldn't see over the horizon because nobody can see over the horizon, not even the humans in the hotel.

After his tiring journey up the breakfast room window and round the gutter on to the warm orange tiles of the roof, he had rested for a short time next to a satellite dish. Now he was ready to find a cosy crack somewhere so he could creep in with his shell and settle down for a snooze.

Before long he found exactly what he'd been looking for, a slightly cracked tile with a raised edge that was just big enough for what he wanted. As he got ready to slide in, a shadow passed over him, blotting out the scorching sun. Socrates quickly pulled his head back into his shell and peeked up to the sky with a rather anxious look on his face. He knew exactly what he didn't want to see.

To his horror, a great black and white seagull was swirling around above him. It didn't exactly have a knife and fork in its webbed feet but by the look on its beak it was clearly ready for some lunch. And Socrates had a really bad feeling that he was the starters.

Oh dear, he thought, I hope I can get under this broken tile before Mr. C. Gull decides to start lunch. It all depends on how fast I, Socrates the sprinting snail of Sorrento, really am.

But would he be fast enough? He would soon know.

Chapter 2

Just before Socrates reached the safety of the broken tile, the black shadow returned. He pulled his head quickly back into his shell. But suddenly he wasn't on the roof of the hotel any more and he could feel himself moving through the air. Plucking up all his courage he peeked carefully out of his shell …. and almost passed out! He was so high up in the sky that everything down on the ground looked like ants, even the humans and their street machines.

However, Socrates was not only the sprinting snail of Sorrento. He was also very, very smart! In fact he was Socrates the smart, sprinting snail of Sorrento, so it didn't take him long to work out exactly where he was. He was tightly clamped in Mr. C. Gull's beak! This wasn't as bad as it sounded because at least he wasn't in Mr. C. Gull's tummy, though he did have an idea that sooner or later that was just where he would end up………… unless he could think of a plan to escape.

Our hero took another look out of the entrance to his shell and he could see the ferry boats that the humans took to go far, far away over the giant puddle to a place he couldn't possibly know. He could also see the hotel where he had started his holiday and he began to wish he'd decided to stay at home under the fridge on the balcony outside the breakfast room. He was also very alarmed to see that, below the hotel, on the bit of the cliff you couldn't see from above, quite a few Mr. C. Gulls and their families were landing and taking off again and making a terrible din.

As he was carried closer and closer to the cliff he saw that most of the black and white birds had little fish in their beaks, little fish that looked awfully unhappy and had really sad faces. Socrates himself was more frightened than sad, but also a little bit relieved because he had expected to have been eaten by now.

Then Mr. C. Gull let him drop. In a flash Socrates realised that it wasn't by accident. The bird wanted to break him out of his shell before having him for lunch. Panic set in as the rocks came hurtling up towards him and he prepared himself for a big "ouch" and a short homeless future.

When the "ouch" came, it wasn't nearly as sore as he had feared but everything began to spin quickly round and round and round. Then there was a sudden splash and he knew at once he was in the big puddle.

His shell had just glanced off the rocks, and as he bobbed along in the water, Socrates felt the black cloud cover him again. He looked around for help and saw only one thing that could save him from another flying lesson. Just an inch away

there was an empty juice can floating on its side.
If he could just reach the hole in the top........

Chapter 3

Mr. C. Gull took careful aim as he swooped down to reclaim his lunch, a rather fancy meal for him after hundreds of little fishes. You can only eat so much fish, you know. His eyes locked on to Socrates, his neck stretched and his beak opened. Splash! He hit the water hard and shot down below the surface before curving his feathered body round and kicking back up. When he got up into the air again, he bobbed around for a moment, trying to work out why his lunch wasn't in his mouth. He looked around with a distinct frown. Where was that snail? It seemed to have disappeared!

Inside the juice can, Socrates held his breath. He was very grateful to the wave that had thrown him inside, just a second before Mr. C. Gull's beak hit the surface of the water. At least for the moment he felt fairly safe. He knew the bird's beak definitely couldn't get into the opening in the top of the can, especially when it was floating on its side. So he was able to watch as Mr. C. Gull flew away lunchless, leaving the teardrop window pointing straight at the hotel he had just left, though it seemed like years ago.

He sat up in his shell as it floated inside the half-filled can and started to plan ahead once more. It took him a long time to figure out how he was going to get home because he didn't know how to make the can go where he wanted it to go. But as long as the hotel kept floating past the window every so often, he hoped the tide would simply take him back to the shore. Then he might be able to sneak through the pebbles and climb the cliff back to the hotel.

Socrates dozed off. He was tired after nearly getting eaten twice. Well so would you be! When he woke up he could sense that the can was moving in a different way and he couldn't see out of the hole in the top. It was covered by something wriggly that seemed to stop wriggling for a while then start swishing from side to side again. And then, as the water began to drain from his holiday home in the can, Socrates realised he wasn't in the water any more. When he rolled to the window to take a closer look, all he could see were fish! Thousands of them, all fighting with each other and climbing over each other, squirming and shivering and curling their tails and opening and closing their mouths gasping for water!

Despite being a very clever sprinting snail of Sorrento, Socrates had no idea where he was.

Chapter 4

There was a sudden whoosh sound and Socrates felt his juice can fall downwards, accompanied by a thousand sad-eyed fish. Luckily for him, his tin home bounced off to the side, just before his unfortunate new friends clattered higgledy-piggledy to a hard wooden floor. And even more luckily, the can bounced right into a tall ring of coiled-up rope where it at last came to rest.

Socrates stayed tucked up in his shell and thought about what had recently happened to him. Almost all of the water had now drained from the juice can through the hole in the top. That meant he could, if he wanted, go for a slither outside and try to find out exactly where he was. He couldn't hear any sign of Mr. C. Gull or his pals, so he assumed it was safe. Those pesky birds usually made an awful racket, especially at lunch and dinner times.

Feeling a lot more optimistic about things in general, Socrates pulled himself through the hole in the can and slid over to the wall of the coil of rope. He felt like a gladiator in the arena, something he'd learned about in snail school. Oh dear! By now the holidays could be over and he would have missed his lessons. That wasn't good, even though he was Socrates the sprinting snail of Sorrento. Lessons were very important. The more a snail knew, the longer it usually lived.

He looked upwards and began to work things out. He had just finished his sums and reckoned he could climb to the top of the coil in ten minutes human time or a week snail time when a yellow rubber monster called Marigold came plunging down. It grabbed the can that had saved his life before pulling it back up and out of sight. "Bye bye caravan life!" Socrates chuckled, for he was a very philosophical snail and he still had a great sense of humour.

He eventually decided that there was really no point in staying where he was for the rest of his life, so he made up his mind to climb up the rings of rope, even though they kept swaying this way and that, as if they were on a see-saw.

Socrates took a deep breath and slid up the first of the many coils that towered above him.

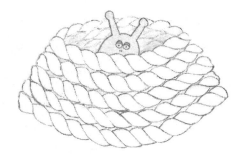

What would he see when he reached the top?

Chapter 5

Climbing the rings of rope proved to be absolutely no problem to our snail friend Socrates as the surface was nice and rough and he had really great suckers. There was no chance of him falling at all, even though he began to feel a tiny bit sick with all the swaying the world was doing. What was causing everything to tilt one way and then the other? For once, Socrates couldn't explain what had happened to him. However he quite soon reached the top coil and was able to peek over it carefully to see where he was.

The first things his eyes saw were the fish. They were all still shivering about, flicking first one way then the other and repeatedly curling their tails up, but not as much as they had been doing when he first met them. Their mouths kept opening and closing as if they were all singing a sad, silent song. Above them hung a great big net with its bottom open as if a pair of giant scissors had snipped it away.

Suddenly, Socrates heard a thud and looked to his right. Now there were more fish lying there, in fact just fish heads – without any bodies. These fish heads just stared at each other. With each new thud, another one fell down from above, joining its expressionless companions. This was not pleasant for our adventurous snail to see so he turned his head back towards the others. The fish that still had both their heads and their bodies looked very unhappy indeed and their big eyes seemed to be asking Socrates to help in some way.

Wanting to help if he possibly could but not exactly sure how, he looked around him and realised that they were on one of those boats he had seen from the hotel, the kind that went right up to the horizon, getting smaller and smaller until they disappeared altogether. He was on a fishing boat! That's why the world kept swaying from side to side. Although he felt really sorry for his fishy companions and wanted to tell them not to worry, Socrates was quite glad that it was they who were getting all the attention and not him.

The sprinting snail of Sorrento could do nothing but give them one last farewell smile then he turned and climbed head-first back down the rope wall. On the way down he chanced upon one or two delicious bits of seaweed stuck in the coils so Socrates had his first meal in what felt like ages. Very soon however, the combination of a big meal upside down and the constant swaying of the boat left him feeling quite nauseous. Luckily he knew that a nice snooze usually cured most bad feelings so he squeezed in between the bottom two coils, put his suckers on auto-suck and fell fast asleep.

When Socrates awoke, the swaying had stopped.

Chapter 6

A quick glance around told our friend Socrates why the world was no longer swaying from side to side: he was out of the boat and back on dry land. He had slept so soundly that he simply hadn't felt the coils of rope being picked up and thrown onto the quayside. And that was why he no longer had the protection or the hiding-place that had kept him safe on the fishing boat. The coils were now all unwound and he could feel the heat of the blazing sun against his thin shell, making him distinctly uncomfortable.

Instinct told him to look for some shade, preferably a nice, quiet place with no human feet stamping about and no cousins of Mr. C. Gull looking for a tasty snack. So Socrates turned off his suckers and slithered off the rope, moving swiftly (by snail standards at least!) towards a large wooden basket. It had orange string walls and no-one appeared to be paying any attention to it. When he reached the basket, he found to his surprise that someone was inside. Looking just as sad as all his fish friends - or should that be ex-friends - was a large grey-blue lobster, and there was another one in a similar basket just to the side.

Socrates introduced himself and politely asked why the lobsters were in baskets on the quayside in the hot sun when they would be much more comfortable back home at the bottom of the sea. The nearer of the two lobsters told the sprinting snail of Sorrento that they were the Cray brothers, inseparable since they were nippers, but that things had taken a turn for the worse when they popped into the two baskets that appeared outside their rock house that very morning. One of the Cray brothers grabbed the orange string wall with both his huge claws and shook with all his might to break free, but it was no use. He looked down at Socrates and explained that they couldn't get out of the baskets because, believe it or not, the doors were one-way. You could get in but you couldn't get out.

Socrates promised to try to help but he kept to himself that he hadn't been of much use to the poor fish on the boat. Still, he slid around the basket looking for a way out for the lobster. By a marvellous stroke of luck he found a string that was broken on the side nearest the water. He shouted to the lobster to try and squeeze out through the hole that was there. He held his breath as Mr. Cray Number 1 worked his claws into the gap and pushed for all he was worth. Ping! A second string broke making the hole even bigger. The lobster was now able to clamber out of the basket and escape.

Much to his surprise, Socrates watched as the lobster slid over the edge of the quayside and plopped into the water where it disappeared from sight in an instant. Not even a thanks and bye

bye! What about his brother? What about being inseparable? Our snail (now feeling a bit of a hero) turned to offer the same help to Mr. Cray 2, but as he did so, the second basket was picked up by one of the fishermen and the lobster was gone. Socrates pondered for a moment on the amazing strokes of fortune that determine what happens to you. Then he realised he wasn't particularly safe himself so he headed for a gap in the cobblestones he had noticed earlier.

Safely inside with only an ant or two for company, Socrates heard the sound of another boat docking nearby, a walkway being laid down from the boat to the quayside and several humans coming ashore. A gigantic suitcase was placed carefully down just where Socrates was hiding. He decided at once to steal a ride on it, in the hope of ending up back at the Regina hotel in Sorrento, so without delay he slithered up and on to the bottom edge of the suitcase. However, for some strange reason this case did not feel good to him, so off he slid and made for a brown leather bag sitting right next to the suitcase. This bag felt a lot more comfortable to our friend Socrates so he stuck himself onto it just out of sight.

No sooner had he engaged auto-suck than the bag was pulled up off the ground and he heard the owner say that he was happy to carry it himself.

"Only if you're quite sure, Mr. Beckham" came the reply.

Chapter 7

Socrates felt Mr. Beckham carry the bag along the quayside while dozens of humans shouted "David, this way!" and took lots of photographs of him. He guessed that Mr. Beckham must be someone really well-known to the humans so he stayed sucked on to the bag in the hope he might end up back at the Regina Hotel. Just where the water met the land, the bag was put down on the back of an electric car. Socrates and Mr. Beckham were whisked up a very steep hill, right to the top so you could see the water on all sides, then along a narrow path where the buggy stopped outside some big iron gates. Like magic, the gates slowly opened all by themselves and in they went.

When the buggy stopped, Socrates could see he was outside a huge, white house with a swimming pool in front of it. Over the wall to the side, he could see the water way down below. He was so high up that Mr. C. Gull and his cousins were actually flying below him! At that moment, the bag was picked up and Socrates was taken into the big, white house, carried up some stairs and put down in a room with a very deep carpet. Without a moment of hesitation, he unstuck himself from the bag and wriggled down into the carpet as deep as he could go.

At the very bottom, Socrates discovered some tiny crumbs of things to eat, so quickly had himself a meal, not knowing when the next one would come along. Common sense told him to make his way through the carpet's woolly trees until he was against the wall and there was little danger of being stood on. This decision proved to be a clever one when four human children came bursting into the room chasing a football which they kicked around until Mr. Beckham told them to go play outside. He must be the Dad, thought the sprinting snail of Sorrento.

Socrates spent the rest of the day and all of the night wandering around in the wool forest where he met up with a centipede, a crowd of ants, a beetle called George and a spider with only five legs. He told Socrates that he had lost one of his legs when he was caught by the Great Sucking Machine which roamed the forest every day and he had had to sacrifice his leg to escape. He warned our snail friend to beware of the terrible machine because he had already lost many acquaintances in its greedy mouth. They never, ever came back. Socrates thanked him for the warning and promised to be on the alert.

The following morning he was awakened by the noise of the children again, this time running into the room and jumping on the bed where Mr. Beckham was lying. All the humans then got up and left the room and a strange silence filled the air, a noiseless calm which was only broken when George the beetle shouted to Socrates to slither up the wall and come look out of the window. It took a while, even for a sprinting snail from Sorrento, but when Socrates reached George he was able to see down into the garden where Mr. Beckham was kicking a ball around with the four children. He looked quite good actually!

Just then there was a knock at the door and a small lady came in pulling a strange round machine behind her. She pushed its fingers into two holes in the wall, stood on a button on its top and all hell was suddenly let loose. A dreadful screaming sound filled the bedroom while the lady pushed the head of the machine at the end of a long neck into the carpet. This must be the Great Sucking Machine, thought the snail. Luckily for George and Socrates, the lady made no attempt to suck things up on the windowsill where they were hiding in a corner, but she rampaged through the wool forest three or four times before standing on the button again to make the machine be quiet.

When she had left, taking her terrifying machine with her, and the two had climbed back down, neither Socrates nor George could find any of their other friends, none of the ants at all in fact. As for the spider, well, they found it but now it only had one leg and it didn't reply when they spoke to it, nor did it move. Its four eyes were all closed and it appeared to be in a deep sleep from which it would not waken.

Socrates had had another lucky escape but he began to wonder if he would ever see his beloved Regina hotel in Sorrento again. He was sure that this bedroom was not the safest place to be, so decided to stay near the bag he had been carried in on.

If Mr. Beckham took his bag and left, Socrates intended to go with him.

Chapter 8

After his first encounter with the Great Sucking Machine, our friend the sprinting snail of Sorrento became rather depressed. You see, he just couldn't understand why bad things happened. He had been brought up to believe that he was put on the Earth for a purpose and that he had to try very hard indeed to be nice to those he met. Hurting others was quite out of the question.

In that case, why were Mr. C. Gull and all his cousins always trying to eat him? And why had all his fish friends had their heads cut off? And who was evil enough to invent the Great Sucking Machine? All of that was quite unnecessary, he thought. Life was hard enough trying to avoid being stood on by humans without having to spend your time watching out for bad things that you didn't even know existed.

Socrates decided to put these questions to George the beetle because he seemed to know an awful lot about life in general and appeared to be able to stay one step ahead of the game. He found his friend in a corner, rolling up what looked like a ball of his own mess, but our snail was of course far too polite to ask what he was doing!

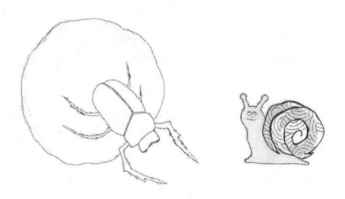

Faced with these difficult problems George chewed things over for a bit and then said that he thought bad things happened to stop life from getting boring! Socrates was rather taken aback with this opinion and he couldn't reply at first. He hadn't expected quite such a simple view of things from such an intelligent beetle. But then George went on to say that it was a complete matter of size whether you were good or bad. Generally speaking, the smaller you were, the less likely you were to be bad because there were fewer things smaller than you to be bad to. The bigger you were, the chances of being bad were much greater, as most things were smaller than you.

Socrates didn't think George's argument made sense. He asked him why you would be bad to something just because it was smaller than you. George laughed and said that obviously you couldn't be bad to something more powerful than yourself! Our snail told him politely that he may be missing the point but George said he didn't mean you *had* to be bad to something smaller than yourself; it was just that you were more likely to. Maybe George wasn't totally comfortable with being asked to explain things, because he decided he'd said enough for one day and scuttled off to do beetle things.

Socrates was puzzled and would have scratched his head if he could have. He settled for withdrawing quietly into his shell for a further think about why being good made more sense to him than being bad. He'd noticed that Mr. Beckham was good to his children and they were much smaller than him. This suggested to Socrates that, just because you were bigger than something, you didn't have to be bad to it. The humans were bigger than most things and they only seemed to be cruel to the other creatures, not other humans. On the other hand, they seemed to be on good terms with dogs and cats like the ones that hung around outside his hotel in Sorrento.

As luck would have it, one of the children came into the room and dropped some food on the carpet but made no attempt to pick it up. As soon as the child had gone, Socrates slid over and helped himself to a piece of nut and a slab of brown stuff which tasted quite delicious. When he had eaten all he wanted, he sprinted back to the edge of the carpet and crawled half way up the leg of the bed just in case the Great Sucking Machine should make an appearance.

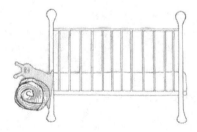

He was learning!

Chapter 9

One night, around midnight, Socrates decided to leave. He quite liked living in the big house with Mr. Beckham and his family but he was constantly worried that the Great Sucking Machine was going to catch him in the middle of the woolly forest. To be honest, he was also fed up waiting for the leather bag to be taken away, giving him a free ride back home.

So, while everyone was asleep, the sprinting snail of Sorrento wriggled over to the big, wooden door, slid underneath and made his way quietly through another woolly forest, this one not quite as deep as the one in the bedroom he had just left. He slithered over to the edge of a long, straight staircase leading down to the ground floor and he could see that the stairs were made of wood and painted shiny white. This meant there would be little problem for him in getting to the front door and out into the open air.

As he paused for a rest next to one of the uprights of the balcony, a small but definite movement caught his eye, something stirring at the bottom of the staircase. He looked closer and could make out in the darkness a hairy shape lying just next to the bottom step. Socrates held in a gasp of fright – it was a dog!

Now, our friend the snail had observed such creatures in the past outside his hotel, the hotel that was as far away as ever, so very far away that it might as well have been on the big, white shape in the night sky, the one the humans called Luna. So he knew that dogs ran around sniffing everything they met and putting lots of things in their slobbery mouths, and he was quite certain he did not want to end up in a dog's mouth any more than he wanted another flying lesson in Mr. C. Gull's beak. It was just too dangerous to go any further, so he gently slid himself behind the base of an upright with a good view of the stairs, hallway and front door, withdrew into his shell and went back to sleep.

A sudden flurry of noisy activity roused Socrates from a strange dream in which he was lying relaxing behind the fridge outside the breakfast room on the balcony of his hotel in Sorrento, but in the company of a second snail which seemed to be another one of himself! However our snail hero had no time to think about this unusual dream because, even as he stretched his feelers and gave a big yawn, he saw the leather bag being carried out of the bedroom, past him and down the stairs where it was put down again at the bottom. He had missed his transport home! Mr. Beckham was already bending down to pick it up again, having said Arrivederci to the lady with the Great Sucking Machine. At that very moment a child's voice came in from the opened front door saying it had left its favourite toy upstairs. Mr. Beckham groaned and then jogged back up the stairs past

Socrates. He disappeared into the room on the right.

Our hero checked that there was now no-one around, neither human, animal nor machine. He calculated he had one chance, one only, and if he missed it he might never get home. Sliding at full speed to the edge of the top stair, he took a deep breath and switched off auto-suck. Plink! Plink! Plink! went the shell as it hit step after step, picking up speed and bouncing higher each time. Inside, Socrates had his feelers wrapped tightly around his eyes and was whispering a prayer for good luck.

With a shuddering whack, the shell, remarkably still in one piece, came to an abrupt halt. Socrates had no time to think. He stuck his head out of the shell and almost cried when he realized he had been stopped by the leather bag just as he had hoped. In a snail's flash he was back on auto-suck, in almost exactly the same position as when he'd met Mr. Beckham for the first time down by the big puddle. He stuck himself once more to the rim at the bottom edge of the bag.

Full of happiness and relief, he felt the ground shudder as Mr. Beckham skipped downstairs with a grinning plastic spaceman in one of his hands. He bent down and Socrates felt the bag rise into the air.

With a bit of luck he was going home!

Chapter 10

With his head full of thoughts of cosying under the fridge on the balcony of the Regina Hotel in Sorrento, Socrates let himself be carried outside. He expected that the electric motor car which had brought them all up to the top of the island of Capri would be waiting to take them back down again. But these homely thoughts were banished at once by the terrible noise that began as they went out of the door. The noise was so awful that our snail friend pulled himself as far back into his shell as he could manage and pulled his horns in so that they almost weren't there any more. Even that didn't blot out the roaring.

The noise was accompanied by a terrible wind that whipped Mr. Beckham's hair all over the place and made the children turn their faces away from the direction they were moving in, something they were finding quite difficult to do. Socrates peered out of the opening in his shell and saw they were all going towards a different kind of machine, a bit like a car but with a twirling thing on top. This was what was causing both the wind and the noise. It was one of the small flying machines he had often seen in the sky from the balcony of his hotel in Sorrento. It was a helicopter!

In next to no time, our friend, the sprinting snail of Sorrento, was wedged next to a glass door, watching the land get further and further away as the helicopter rose higher and higher into a cloudless, blue sky. Then it swung out over the sea, the one Socrates must have travelled over in the fishing boat. Heart pounding faster and faster with the excitement of his latest flight – and certainly one less worrying than his other journey in the beak of Mr. C. Gull – the snail looked far ahead to the approaching shoreline. Wait a minute! Was that the hotel he could see? His own hotel? The Regina Hotel? He pulled himself forward out of his shell for a better view and almost screamed with delight when he realised the helicopter was heading straight for his home.

Socrates was in a spin, wondering how he was going to tell all his friends back at snail school about his amazing adventures on the island of

Capri, about his scrapes with Mr. C. Gull, the fishing boat, Mr. Beckham, the Great Sucking Machine and George the philosopher beetle.

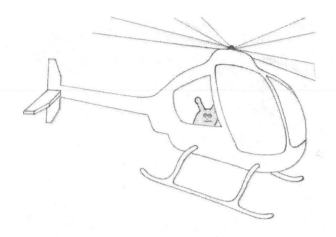

He looked out of the glass door once again just to be sure they were at the right place and, yes, they were nearly there, only a short distance from his home. He could even see one of the waiters, Giovanni, serving some of the customers in the breakfast room at the top of the building. And look! There was his fridge! He was home!

Suddenly, Socrates felt the helicopter tilt to one side so that he was now looking straight up into the air. Mr. Beckham's children all squealed with pretend fright as they were pushed over in their seats although they were all tightly strapped in. But when they levelled off and Socrates could see the shoreline again, his hotel had gone! They were flying away from it faster than ever. Our snail friend's eyes filled with tears again, but this time the tears were sad ones, as he realised they weren't going to the Regina Hotel after all. They were going somewhere else, somewhere he had probably never heard of, somewhere that wasn't Sorrento. Broken hearted, Socrates checked his auto-suck and cried himself to sleep.

When he awoke, he saw he was still on Mr. Beckham's bag and it was still moving, but now it was moving all by itself! No-one was carrying it! Instead it was rolling along a bumpy table and heading for a huge set of black curtains which he passed through, clinging on for all his life. Inside it was very dark and there was a deep, growling sound. Socrates found himself feeling very strange and for an instant his auto-suck almost switched off by itself. Luckily, just at that moment, the bag came back out from the dark tunnel with our snail still on board.

Socrates watched in amazement as Mr. Beckham came over, picked up the bag, turned around to let hundreds of people take flashy photos of him (and him!) then carried the bag over to another flying machine. He climbed into it and a small door made of steps closed behind him. The bag was then shoved into a kind of cupboard above Mr. Beckham's head and that was that. Our snail could feel lots of movement and hear some sounds, such as the children speaking to their Dad, but he could see absolutely nothing except the inside of the box. There was nothing left to do but wait.

Clunk! Suddenly the box was open again and this time someone else grabbed the bag and carried it to the door of the flying machine, the door that had turned back into steps. Outside, Socrates could see thousands of people waving and cheering while Mr. Beckham waved back and smiled. The crowds had coloured flags with "PSG" written on them and on a building nearby there was a great big banner that read "Bienvenu à Paris, David. Je t'adore!" Now you'd be surprised if a sprinting snail from Sorrento could speak French, but Socrates at least recognized the name of the city on the banner.

He was in Paris, the capital of France. The country where the people love to eat snails!

THE END

Made in the USA
Charleston, SC
29 November 2016